Marvelous Magical Stories

KINGFISHER

BOSTON

KINGFISHER
a Houghton Mifflin Company imprint
222 Berkeley Street
Boston, Massachusetts 02116
www.houghtonmifflinbooks.com

First published in 2007
2 4 6 8 10 9 7 5 3 1

LIBRARY OF CONGRESS CATALOGING-IN-PUBLICATION DATA
has been applied for.

ISBN 978-0-7534-6072-6

Printed in China
1TR/0507/PROSP/MAR/80NEWSP/C

SUPER SHORTS

Marvelous Magical Stories

compiled by Elizabeth Holland

KINGFISHER

BOSTON

Contents

Chantelle, the Princess Who Couldn't Sing

Joyce Dunbar

Once upon a time there was a princess named Chantelle. She was as beautiful as she was good, as good as she was graceful, and as graceful as she was kind. But the most enchanting thing about her was her voice, and people loved to hear her sing.

When the princess reached the age

of 15, a party was held in her honor. All of the guests came with good wishes. All except one—an ill-tempered aunt who was jealous of Chantelle. "Why should this slip of a princess have so much?" she grumbled to herself. And instead of giving her a good wish, this jealous aunt cast a spell so that when the princess started to sing, her beautiful voice was spirited away and let loose out a window.

"There," cackled the aunt. "Sing away!"

From that day on, the princess could not sing at all. Not a high note nor a low note, not a *la-la* nor a *tra-la*: whenever she tried to sing, the sound that came out of her beautiful throat was flat, as flat as a doormat.

"I can't understand it," said the queen.

"She used to have such a sweet voice," said the king.

As for Chantelle herself, it was clear from the way that she screeched and squawked so happily around the palace that she simply did not realize it. She had become completely tone-deaf. The king and queen hired the best music teachers, but they all gave up in despair. And rather than offend her by telling her to be quiet, the king and queen and courtiers covered their ears.

Now, it so happened that a handsome prince came to seek Chantelle's hand in marriage. He had heard all about the beautiful princess with the beautiful voice who loved to sing so much. But because no one talked about it, he hadn't heard that she could no longer sing.

As soon as the prince and princess met, they immediately fell in love with each other and get engaged. A celebration banquet was held, and everyone ate, drank, and was merry. It seemed that there could never be a happier couple.

At the end of the banquet, the prince turned to the king. "Your majesty," he said, "I cannot tell you how happy I am to be marrying your lovely daughter, who is so renowned for her lovely voice. You know that my court is famous for its music, and as you can see I have brought my lyre. What could be a more fitting end to this occasion than that the princess should accompany me in a song?"

An embarrassed silence fell upon the court. But the princess wasn't embarrassed, not at all. Smiling, she rose to her feet. The prince began to play, and the princess opened her mouth to sing . . . but, oh, what a dreadful noise she made—it was flat, as flat as a doormat.

The prince stopped his playing in astonishment. Then a pageboy began to giggle, then a serving maid, until the whole court fell over laughing. But this was no joke. While the princess trembled and blushed crimson, the prince frowned. He could not possibly take such a princess as his bride—she would turn his court into a laughingstock! Muttering his excuses, the prince decided to return home. "I'll come back in a month," he said, "but make sure that the princess has some singing lessons."

Poor Chantelle ran from the palace in tears. She found a hiding place among the bulrushes that grew by the royal lake and sobbed and sobbed, until at last a frog heard her and asked what was the matter.

"A handsome prince wants to marry me, and he asked me to sing for him. But he didn't like my singing. Neither did anyone else. I can no longer sing a note," she sobbed.

"Don't you worry," said the frog. "I have a very fine voice myself. Meet me every morning at daybreak, and I'll soon teach you how to sing again."

And so, at dawn for a month, the princess had singing lessons from the frog. She made excellent progress, and when the prince made his promised return, the frog told her that she was sure to please him.

Once more a banquet was held, and this time the prince brought his lute. He plucked a few notes, and the princess began to sing. But the sound that came out of her beautiful mouth was . . . well . . . a passionate, full-throated C-R-o-A-K!

Of course the whole court fell

over laughing—all except the frog king, who followed the sound from the royal pond and immediately fell in love with the princess.

Again, the prince made his excuses, promising to return in a month, while Chantelle ran away in tears. She hid herself in a rose arbor and sobbed and croaked her heart out, until the kitchen cat came by and asked her what was the matter.

"I'm in love with a handsome prince who wants to marry me. But first I must learn to sing, as I can no longer sing a note."

"Don't you worry about that," said

the kitchen cat.
"I have the best voice for
miles around. Meet me at
moonrise each evening,
and I'll soon teach you
how to sing again."

And so, by the light of the moon,
the princess had singing lessons from
the kitchen cat. At the end of the
month he pronounced her perfectly
in pitch and said that she was sure to
please the prince this time.

Well, you can imagine what
happened. The prince began to play
his flute, and the princess started to
sing. But the sound that came from

her mouth was an ear-piercing,
spine-shattering H-O-W-L!

And the court laughed until their
sides ached. The prince did not laugh,
but departed as before, vowing that
he would give the princess only one
more chance. And the king of cats did
not laugh either. He followed the
sound from the other side of the forest
and immediately fell in love with her.

This time the princess ran away to a

forest where she could cry her heart out in peace. But she woke up an owl, who asked her what was the matter.

The princess told her story. "We'll soon put that right," said the owl. "I've got a voice that charms the birds off the trees. Meet me at midnight every night, and I'll soon teach you how to sing once more."

So, every midnight in the forest, the princess took singing lessons from the owl.

"There," said the owl at last. "You, too, can charm the birds off the trees. You should certainly be able to charm a prince."

At the next banquet, when the princess opened her beautiful mouth to sing, the sound that came from her throat was the shrillest, sharpest TOO-WHIT-TOO-WHOO!

Although they tried to stop themselves, everyone fell off their chairs, howling and hooting with laughter. They laughed until the tears rolled down their cheeks, cruel tears of mockery. How the princess blushed! How humiliated she felt!

But the owl king in the forest heard her and fell right off his treetop in love.

This time the princess ran so far into the dark forest that she was lost.

Now, this part of the forest was enchanted, and it was there that the princess, worn out with misery and hunger, fell asleep.

The frog king eyed her from an enchanted pool. The king of cats gazed at her from beside an enchanted stone. The owl king blinked at her from an enchanted tree.

Then a strange sound began, a clear and beautiful sound. It was a human voice! It sang so finely and so sweetly, a melody as light as air, that it woke up the princess. Although Chantelle did not know it, it was her own voice. Stolen by

the ill-tempered aunt and let loose out the window, the voice had sung its way to the enchanted forest. Now it worked its charm on the princess, and she could truly hear again.

"Oh, I would give everything to have a voice like that," the princess said with a sigh.

"Be mine and you will!" croaked

the frog king, wishing that she was a frog.

"Be mine and you will!" howled the king of cats, wishing that she was a cat.

"Be mine and you will!" hooted the owl king, wishing that she was an owl.

In that instant the lovely voice was hers again. But in this enchanted forest, wishes had a dangerous way of coming true. As she sang, she changed. She lost her human form. Instead, she was the color of a frog, with the fur of a cat, and the shape of an owl! Only her eyes were her own.

The owl king screeched in dismay, the frog king croaked in disgust, and the king of cats slunk away in distaste. When Chantelle went to drink from the enchanted pool, she wept to see what she had become.

Now she could sing better than any human being alive to the lyre, to the

lute, and to the flute. But what prince would want her now? What use would she be to anyone? With her own wings, she soared through the forest, her singing more beautiful by day than the lark's and more beautiful by night than the nightingale's.

It so happened that the very same prince went hunting with his men in the forest one day. He was full of remorse at the disappearance of Princess Chantelle and had given up all hope of finding her. So, when he heard this beautiful voice, he made a vow.

"I gave up the princess I loved for a voice," he said to his men. "Now, here is a beautiful voice. Whoever owns it, whether she is young or old, wise or foolish, fair or foul, I will marry her. Catch her by whatever means you can." And because it was an enchanted forest, where wishes strangely came true, the huntsmen caught Chantelle in the first trap that they set and brought her before the prince, so changed that he did not know her.

She sat in a gilded cage, singing and singing, a creature so weird and

wonderful that the prince
could only stare at her
in appalled fascination.
But a prince must keep his word.
Without further ado, he
married the strange
creature and took her back
to the palace.

But she did not sit on
the throne as his princess.
Instead, she was locked
in a tower at the
very top of the
palace, there to
sing her heart
out, filling the

palace and its grounds with her beautiful melodies. The prince listened and was enchanted, for in the sound was a vision of the beautiful Princess Chantelle.

"If only I had married her," he kept saying to himself. "How happy I should be! But I asked for everything. So now I have my just reward. I am married to a voice, nothing but a voice. I have to make the best of it."

Because the prince could not bear to look at the strange creature, he hired a keeper to take care of her. And it happened that this keeper was none other than the ill-tempered aunt who had cast the spell on the princess. She recognized the eyes and the voice of Chantelle, and she had an evil thought.

"What a waste of a handsome prince! What a waste of a beautiful voice! If only I could steal the voice for myself, the prince might marry me instead. But first I must get rid of this monster."

She fed poisoned food to the strange creature, day after day, little by little, until at last the creature fell into a deep sleep from which nothing could awaken it.

"We must take it

back to the heart of the forest where we found it," said the prince. "There, it might revive."

They went in a solemn procession, the princess carried on a bier to the middle of the enchanted forest and the ill-tempered aunt keeping watch.

"One last dose of poison," she said to herself, "and all that is hers will be mine."

But the owl king in his treetop heard her. The frog king on his lily pad heard her. The king of cats in the undergrowth heard her.

"You want what the princess has," they said, "and you will have it!"

Because this was a place where wishes had a dangerous way of coming true, no sooner was this uttered than the strange creature turned back into Princess Chantelle, as warm and alive and human as on the last day that the prince had seen her. At the same time, the ill-tempered aunt's neck began to bulge like a frog's, her voice began to hiss like a cat's, and her face became as sharp as an owl's. She screamed with rage and tore through the forest, never to be seen again.

The prince looked at his beloved princess and said, "What a fool I have been. Can you ever forgive me?"

Princess Chantelle did forgive him, and when she opened her mouth to sing, the sound that came out of her beautiful throat was the voice that had been let loose in the enchanted forest. It was her own true voice, so happy to have found its owner that it *la-laad* and *tra-laad* as merrily as could be.

The Magical Apple Tree
Judy Hindley

Rosy lived with a mean old wicked witch. The witch did nothing at all but count her money.

Rosy did all of the work.

She fed the hens that laid eggs for the witch.

She fed the cow that gave milk to the witch.

She fed the horse that pulled the

cart that carried the wood for the witch's fire.

All summer she grew corn and hay and oats to fill the barns for the animals' winter food.

But the witch sold the corn and hay and oats and kept the money.

When the winter came, there was no food in the barns.

The hens were so hungry that they laid no more eggs.

The cow was so hungry that it gave no more milk.

And the poor old horse was too weak to pull the cart.

The witch said, "YOU'RE NO USE NOW. Tomorrow morning the hens will go in the cooking pot, and the cow will go to the butcher. That old horse can go wherever it likes— and so can you!"

She kicked Rosy out into the snow and slammed the door. Then she laughed her wicked laugh and said, "Caw, caw, caw!" just like a mean old crow.

Rosy cried, but the hungry animals gathered around her.

So she said, "I must go on. After

all, crying won't help, and trying might help." She picked up her empty basket and went away into the cold, bare woods.

Rosy walked and walked till she came to an apple tree. It called to her. In a sad little voice it cried, "Please, dear Rosy, shake me, shake me, or this heavy fruit will break me!"

Rosy looked up. All she saw was one dead leaf. But the tree cried, "Shake me, shake me!" So she did.

Suddenly, it was covered with yellow apples! Rosy filled her basket and hurried home.

As she went, the basket got heavier and heavier.

But she didn't stop for a minute till she got home.

She tipped out the fruit, and the animals crowded around.

None of them saw that the last five apples had turned to gold.

But the witch did. "AHA!" she cried. "WHO DID YOU ROB?"

"No one," said Rosy. "I found these apples in the woods. There were lots and lots."

"LOTS?" cried the witch. And she rushed into the woods.

Through the bare trees, the magical apple tree glimmered with fruit.

But the witch pushed past it.

"Please," cried the apple tree, "shake me, shake me, or this heavy fruit will break me!"

But the witch said, "Poo! I'm looking for golden apples. Shake yourself!"

So it did.

But this time, the apples turned into stones.

"Ow, ow, ow!" cried the witch.
She hopped and flapped, just like a
mean old crow.

And suddenly the wind picked her
up and whirled her away. And she
never came back.

But Rosy sold the golden apples
and was rich! And she and the
animals never went hungry again.

The Three Wishes

The Brothers Grimm

There was once a poor man who had
a very pretty wife. They were so poor
that they hardly had enough to eat
and hardly enough wood to make a
fire. But one winter evening the man
came in with a shiny brass coal scuttle,
piled high with coal. "Look what I
found by the door," he said to his wife.
"It must be a gift. We will have a

good blaze tonight."

They sat down
to warm
themselves,
and the wife
began to talk
about the

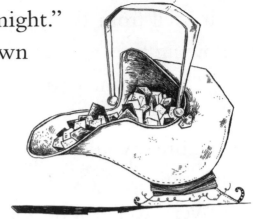

neighbors. "They are happier than
we are because they are richer," said
the wife. "But if only we could meet
a fairy who would grant us a wish,
we would be happier and richer than
all of them."

"That would be a fine thing," said
her husband.

No sooner had they spoken than a

fairy fell from the embers of the glowing fire.

"I will grant you a wish," said the fairy.

"Three would be better," said the wife.

"Very well, then," said the fairy, "three wishes. But only three wishes. I will grant you nothing more." And with that, she faded away.

The man and his wife settled down to decide what to wish for. "I will not make a wish yet," said the wife, "but I think nothing could be better than an embroidered silk purse, full of gold."

"What a silly wish," said her husband. "Why, you could wish for ten silk purses, twenty, or even a hundred. But what use would they be to you if you were sick? It would be much better to wish for health, happiness, and a long life."

"But what is the use of a long life if you are poor? It only makes the misery last longer. Now that I come to think of it, that fairy should have granted us a dozen wishes. Then we could have everything we want."

"That's true," said her husband. "But never mind. If we take our time and think carefully, we will make the most of our three wishes."

"I will think all night and make up my mind in the morning," said his wife. "Meanwhile, let us warm ourselves by the fire, for it is very cold." She poked the fire until it flared up very nicely, but her belly rumbled with hunger. "Ah," she said and sighed, without thinking. "What a splendid fire. I wish we had a piece of black pudding to cook on it for our supper."

She had hardly said these words

when *clitter-clatter* down the chimney came a piece of black pudding, more than enough for two.

Her husband was furious. "You greedy pig!" he shouted. "What a waste of a good wish! Why, I wish that black pudding was attached to the end of your nose!"

He soon felt sorry that he had spoken, for the black pudding jumped up immediately and stuck fast on the end of his pretty wife's nose.

"Owwww! What have you done?" wailed the wife. "Get it off!"

Her husband gave it a pull, but it stuck. Then she gave it a pull, but it

stuck. Then they
both pulled so
hard that they
almost pulled
off her nose,
but it was really,
really stuck.

"I'm sorry, wife,"
said the husband. "But
what if I was to wish for that
embroidered silk purse, after all? You
could use it to hide the black pudding."

"Owwww!" wailed the wife. "I
should hide my head in that coal
scuttle. How could I bear to be seen
with a black pudding dangling from

the end of my nose, even with a silk purse to hide it? Oh, I wish that it would drop off."

That very instant, the black pudding dropped off the wife's nose.

"There goes our last wish," groaned her husband.

"Owwww! Owwww! Owwww!" wailed the wife.

But she sat down and thought for a while, until at last she came to her senses. "It serves us right. We asked for too much, and this is how the fairy has punished us. From now on we should count our blessings. See! We have a shiny brass coal scuttle

half full of coal.
We have a black
pudding. That
is more than
we had to

begin with. Why don't we sit here
by the warm fire and cook the black
pudding for our supper?"

And they did. And, oh, it was good.

The Cletterkin

Jenny Koralek

One morning after breakfast, Leggie
Meggie ran into the yard to play with
her new, yellow, very small bouncy
ball. And after one bounce, she lost it.
She rushed inside calling, "Mom! Dad!
Granny! I've lost my new best ball!"

"I can't help you now," said Dad
angrily. "I've lost my car keys. I will
have to walk to work, and I'll be

very late."

"What we need in this house," said Granny, "is a cletterkin."

But Dad didn't hear. He had left, banging the door behind him.

"And I can't help you," said Mom. "I've lost my glasses. I've hunted high and low. I won't be able to read my book on the way to work, and I'll be late too."

"What we need in this house," said Granny, "is a cletterkin."

But Mom didn't hear. She had left, banging the door behind her.

Leggie Meggie heard, though.

"What's a cletterkin?" she asked.

Granny looked up from her knitting. "A cletterkin finds things," she said, "and organizes what's disorganized. A cletterkin can see into all of the little nooks and crannies, inside and out, where balls roll and car keys fall and glasses lie. When I was a little girl every house had a cletterkin."

"What does a cletterkin look like?" asked Leggie Meggie. "I've never seen one myself," said

Granny. She stopped to pick up a stitch from her knitting. "But . . ."

"But what?" asked Leggie Meggie.

"Once I met a man who'd met a man who said . . . a cletterkin has furry feet and leafy hair. He moves on feet as soft as cats' paws. He can shoot up as tall as a tree and shrink as small as a mouse. And because he can hunt high and low, he can find high and low. I never saw the cletterkin in our house, but I know, I just know that he was the one who always found my lost penny and my brother's best blue marble."

"What was that noise?" asked Leggie Meggie.

"What noise?" said Granny.

"Soft on the floorboards, like cats' paws," said Leggie Meggie.

"I didn't hear anything," Granny said, yawning. "And now, oh dear, I've lost my knitting needle. I tell you, what we need in this house is a cletterkin."

She yawned again and began to nod off in her chair.

Leggie Meggie went back into the yard to look for her ball. She looked in the long grass. She looked under the bushes. She found a stick and poked around in the stinging nettles. Where could it be?

"Maybe it fell into one of the flowerpots," she said. She looked in three flowerpots. They were empty, except one that had a little bed of dry leaves and some snail shells full of raindrops. She was just about to put her hand into another flowerpot when a voice said, "Didn't you know, long-leggedy, it's very rude to scramble around in people's houses? You've just unmade my bed and tipped over my cups."

There, by the flowerpot with the
bed of dry leaves and the snail shells
full of raindrops, was a little man with
leafy hair and furry feet. He was
sitting on Leggie Meggie's new,
yellow, very small bouncy ball.

"A cletterkin!" cried Leggie
Meggie. "Just like Granny said!"

"Not *a* cletterkin," said the little man.
"*The* cletterkin, the last cletterkin."

"What happened to the others?"
asked Leggie Meggie.

"They went away long ago to look
for the rainbow's end," said the
cletterkin.

"Oh, dear," said Leggie Meggie.

"They'll never find it."

"I know," the cletterkin said with
a sigh.

"Don't be sad," said Leggie
Meggie. "We need you in our house.
Granny says so, because we're always
losing things. Just in one morning
I've lost my ball, Dad's lost his car
keys, Mom's lost her glasses, and
Granny's lost her knitting needle!
Oh, won't you be our cletterkin?"

"Well," said the cletterkin briskly,
"you do sound like a very messy
family!" But he made that sound like
something good. "If you've lost all
those things since you got up this

morning, who knows what you'll
have lost by bedtime? I'd better get
started right away."

So Leggie Meggie led the way
into the house. She showed the
cletterkin the cat flap.

"You can always come in and out
through there," she whispered,

"when I'm not here to let you in. Because we will be secret about you, won't we?"

"Of course," said the cletterkin, "and anyway, I have a little trick. I can make myself invisible if I want to."

"Go on," said Leggie Meggie. Suddenly the cletterkin had vanished, but Leggie Meggie heard his voice singing, "Cletter, cletter, that's better!" Then something scuttered through the newspaper lying like a tent on the floor, and there were Mom's glasses lying at Granny's feet.

"Cletter, cletter, that's better," came a voice from somewhere near the front door. "Car keys in an old boot! There's enough work here for a hundred years."

There was a scurrying of feet as soft as cats' paws, and there were Dad's keys lying at Granny's feet.

"Cletter, cletter, that's better," sang the invisible cletterkin, and Granny's knitting needle seemed to heave itself up from a wide crack in the floorboards.

And there he was, sitting on top of

Granny's knitting basket.

Just then the door banged, and Leggie Meggie heard her mother calling.

"I must go now," she said.

"And I'm off to my house," said the cletterkin.

"I'll come out and play later," whispered Leggie Meggie, and the cletterkin shot out through the cat flap.

When Mom and Dad saw all of the lost things laid out at Granny's feet, they were very pleased.

"Good girl, Leggie Meggie," said Dad.

"It wasn't me," said Leggie Meggie.

"Was it Granny, then?" They smiled at Granny sleeping in her chair. "Dear Granny, no wonder she's tired."

Then Granny woke up. She saw her lost knitting needle neatly placed beside a ball of wool. She saw Leggie Meggie holding her new, yellow, very small bouncy ball. She saw the keys and Mom's glasses lying by her feet.

"Well," she said, "perhaps there is a cletterkin around after all!"

The Wonder Broom

Joyce Dunbar

Philipippa was the kitchen maid in King Carraway's palace. She washed the royal dishes, peeled the royal potatoes, and swept the royal floors.

She did a lot more work besides, for

the royal cook was a bully who never stopped bossing her around.

The royal cook was also very fat. Her cotton print dresses were so tight that it looked as if the buttons might burst at any moment.

One morning, the royal cook sent Philipippa to the market to buy a new broom. "This old one is disgusting, a disgrace to the royal household," she said with annoyance.

"Yes, ma'am," Philipippa answered politely.

It didn't take Philipippa long to get to the market. She tried every stall, but she couldn't find a broom anywhere. She didn't dare go back to the royal palace without one, for then the cook's buttons would surely burst.

She was wondering what to do when a peddler came by. "Wonder brooms! Wonder brooms!" he shouted.

"But you have only one broom," said Philipippa.

"Why, yes. These brooms are so wonderful that I have sold all of the others," lied the peddler. "This is the last one I have left." He didn't tell her that he had found just that one broom on the royal road that very morning!

Philipippa bought the wonder broom

and hurried back to the royal palace.

"Dawdler! What a long time you've been!" the cook scolded.

"Indeed, ma'am, I—"

"Enough of your sauciness!" snapped the cook. "And don't just stand there gawking. Anybody would think that we had nothing to do!

I've been making the stuffing for the royal goose, and the crumbs have gone all over the floor. Sweep the kitchen! Sweep the hall! Sweep the yard!" With that, the cook snatched up a royal saucepan and banged it down on the fire so hard that hot coals shot off in all directions.

My! What a temper she has, thought Philipippa, nervously watching out for buttons.

She picked up the new broom and began sweeping the floor. Over the royal red tiles flew the wonder broom, *swish, swish, swish*. She had no sooner begun than it was done.

Not a crumb nor a hot coal in sight!
Philipippa stared in amazement. It
really was a wonder broom. So light!
It must be enchanted.

"Well, if this isn't my lucky day,"
said Philipippa, patting the broom
affectionately. "We are going to be
great friends, I can see."

The next day, quite early, a crotchety
old woman came
knocking on the
royal kitchen
door. Philipippa
had almost
finished all of
her sweeping

for the morning, so the cook was about to set her scrubbing. But first she had to answer the door.

"May I ask what you are doing with my broom?" snapped the crotchety old woman.

"*Your* broom?" cried Philipippa in astonishment. "Why, I bought it myself at the market yesterday."

"So what if you did?" said the crotchety old woman. "I tell you it is my broom, just the same," and she tried to snatch it away.

"Well, and what about me?" the broom asked suddenly, in a swishy-swooshy voice.

Philipippa was so surprised that she let go of the broom handle with a jerk. It didn't fall, but stood all by itself in the middle of the floor!

"Come here at once!" cackled the crotchety old woman. "How dare you run away like that?"

"Run away yourself," piped the broom, "you crusty old fussbudget! I am much happier where I am, thank you."

"Oh, are you?" cried

the old woman. "We'll soon see who is the boss around here."

"Oh, will we?" retorted the broom, quivering with rage. "Go away at once, or I'll sweep you out!"

"Oh, you can't do that," said Philipippa.

But no sooner had she spoken than the broom began sweeping as hard as it could go. It swept the old woman out of the kitchen, across the courtyard, and over the palace drawbridge. *Swish, swish, swish!*

The cook came running to see what was the matter.

Swish, swish, swish, went the

broom! *Pop, pop, pop,* went the cook's buttons!

She burst right out of her dress and went running away in her petticoat.

And then, all of a sudden, the broom was back in Philipippa's hands, just as if nothing had happened.

The cook and the crotchety old woman didn't come back, so Philipippa kept the wonder broom. And although she never told anyone the tale, no one ever bullied her again!

The Hedley Kow

Maggie Pearson

What sort of creature is the Hedley Kow? It's not a cow, that's for sure— well, only sometimes. Sometimes it looks like a cow.

Sometimes it looks like a horse— and a very fine horse too, until you try to ride it. Then it's likely to turn itself into a bale of straw, or a pool of water, or . . . You may see the

Hedley Kow and never know it: who's to say?

There was an old woman who made ends meet as best she could. A bit of sewing here. A bit of apple picking there. A bit of mowing in some other place. It was a hard life, but she made the best of it.

One day while she was walking home, she spied what looked like an old cooking pot lying in a ditch.

"Well!" she said. "There's a lucky thing! I daresay the pot has a hole in it, or it wouldn't have been thrown away, but it's just the thing to stand on my window ledge with a pot of flowers inside it." She went and looked at the pot more closely. It was full of gold pieces.

"Well!" she said. "That is a lucky thing! It's a case of finders keepers, I suppose. I shall be able to live in comfort for the rest of my days."

The pot of gold was too heavy to carry, so she tied her shawl around it and began to drag it home.

Even then it was hard work, and after a while she had to stop and rest.

She looked inside the pot again.

"Well!" she said. "It's not gold after all—it's silver. That's even luckier. I wouldn't have been happy with all that gold around the house. There are thieves and there are beggars and there are the neighbors getting jealous. I'll be much better off with silver."

Off she went again, with her shawl tied around the pot, dragging it along behind her.

It wasn't long before she had to
stop and rest again. She went to look
at the silver in the pot and found
that it wasn't a pot at all, but a solid
lump of iron.

"Well!" said the old woman. "I do
get even luckier and luckier! I'd never
have known what to do with all that
silver, for I've never had more than
one silver sixpence at a time in all
my life before. But a lump of iron is
just what I've been needing to prop
open my door so that the sun can
shine straight in."

Off she went again, with her shawl
wrapped around the lump of iron,

dragging it behind her. She didn't stop until she came to her own front door.

Then she bent down to untie the shawl. As soon as she had done so, the lump of iron shook itself, stood up on four long legs, gave a laugh, and went galloping off into the dark.

"Well!" said the old woman. "Isn't that the luckiest thing of all! If I hadn't brought home that old iron pot—that turned out to be full of gold—that turned out to be silver— that turned out to be a lump of iron—I'd never have seen the Hedley Kow with these two eyes of mine. I must be the luckiest old woman alive."

Baby Wizard

Chris Powling

Once there was a Baby Wizard.

Her dad was a wizard, her mom was a wizard, and so was her big brother, aged five, who'd just started Wizard School. They lived in a spiky-towered castle with a deep, dark forest all around it—which is just where you'd expect a wizard family to live.

One thing you wouldn't expect, though. This Baby Wizard was special. She couldn't walk yet. She couldn't talk yet. She couldn't feed herself yet—and she certainly couldn't use her potty.

BUT SHE COULD MAKE MAGIC!

At first, of course, the family didn't believe it.

"Impossible," said her dad. "Wizards must *learn* how to make magic—no one can be magical while they're still wearing a diaper!"

Baby Wizard could.

"*Goo-goo-goo,*" she said. And instantly she turned her stroller into a racecar that roared straight down the highway as far as the big city. Her mom and dad were furious when they had to get her from the police station.

Mealtimes were even worse. Sometimes Baby Wizard turned her food into rubber so that it bounced all over the castle kitchen. Sometimes she made it so heavy that

it fell to the floor with a CRASH
that shook the whole forest.
Sometimes she floated it out a window
so that it hung high up over the
castle like a tiny, food-colored cloud.

At bath time she was even naughtier
—filling the bathtub with crocodiles,
for instance.

"Crocodiles?" shrieked Mom,

snatching Baby Wizard from the water. "She's too little even to have heard of crocodiles!"

"*Goo-goo-goo*," said Baby Wizard. And the crocodiles changed into dragons that were so fiery that they almost burned the bathroom to pieces with their breath.

Naturally, all of this was a big nuisance—but nothing more than a nuisance. Remember, every member of her family was a wizard. They could always put things right with plenty of magic of their own.

The real problem came at bedtime. Bedtime, yes.

Her mom and dad and her big brother, aged five, were too terrified now to go to sleep. Night after night

they lay awake, wondering what Baby Wizard would get up to after dark.

"Suppose it's a magic sneeze!" exclaimed her dad. "She might blow away the whole forest!"

"Suppose it's a magic burp!" cried

Mom. "She might split the castle in half like an earthquake!"

"Suppose it's a magic nightmare!" yelled her big brother, aged five. "She might fill every corner of the forest with *gho-gho-gho*-ghosts!"

Even when they took turns watching over Baby Wizard's crib, it didn't help. They were still so scared of what might happen that none of them closed their eyes for a moment.

"This is terrible," Baby Wizard's mom said with a yawn. "I can't remember when we last had a good night's sleep."

"We're falling to pieces from

tiredness," Dad groaned. "Isn't there anything we can do?"

Baby Wizard's big brother, aged five, looked down at his little sister in her crib and scratched his head thoughtfully.

"Dad," he said, "can a kitten do magic?"

"*A kitten?*"

"Or a puppy?"

"*A puppy?*"

"Or a chick? Or a calf? Or a piglet?"

"Of course not," Dad Wizard said. "Only a wizard can do magic—you learn how at Wizard School. Or so I thought, until your sister came along."

"That's what I thought," said Baby Wizard's big brother, aged five. "So now I've got the answer to our problem!"

Quickly, he waggled his fingers and muttered a magic word.

"Meow-meow," went Baby Wizard in her sleep. Then, "*Purr-purr-purr.*"

Baby Wizard's big brother, aged five, had turned her into a kitten!

Every bedtime after that, Baby Wizard licked her whiskers, curled

her tail, and purred herself to sleep till morning . . . except, of course, when she'd been turned into a puppy or a chick or a calf or a piglet.

And her family slept happily ever after.

Especially her big brother, aged five, who'd just started Wizard School. Some people say that by the time he's grown up he'll be the best wizard ever . . . unless, of course, his sister is just as good.

The Queen of the Bees

Vivian French

Once there were three sisters who lived in a fine big castle. Their father was a king, and their mother was a queen, so all three were princesses— and very special, the two eldest thought themselves.

"Of course," the eldest princess said, "I am as beautiful as the moon!"

"HUH!" said the second princess.

"YOU? Why, I am as beautiful as the sun!"

"What GARBAGE!" said the eldest, and she stamped her foot.

"EVERYBODY knows that I am the most beautiful!"

"NONSENSE!" shouted the second. "Absolute NONSENSE!"

The king listened, and he shook his head sadly. The queen tut-tutted to herself. The prime minister snorted.

"If you'll excuse me for saying so, your majesties," he said, "I think it's high time those princesses went out on a quest. They'll never find a prince any other way—they're too rude."

"POO!" said the two princesses. "We don't want to do that!"

The youngest princess was helping a butterfly escape out a window. "What's a quest?" she asked.

"You're a ninny!"
said her eldest sister.
"Imagine not knowing
that! It's going out on an
adventure to find your fortune!"

"And breaking a spell and finding
a prince," said the second princess.
"But you're MUCH too stupid ever
to do that."

"Yes," said the eldest, "MUCH too
stupid!"

The prime minister coughed.
"Excuse me, your majesties, but
doesn't that prove my point?"

The king sighed heavily. "You're

quite right," he said. "But is a quest the only way?"

The prime minister nodded. "Yes," he said. "Unless you want them here in the palace forever and ever."

The king and queen looked horrified.

"A quest it will be," said the king.

"At once!" said the queen.

The three princesses were sent off on their quest the very next day. The two eldest moaned and complained bitterly, but the king and queen were firm.

"You can come back as soon as you've finished," said the king.

"As soon as you've found your fortune and broken a spell and found your prince," said the queen. "I'm sure it won't take long." And she waved them goodbye from the top of the castle.

The two eldest princesses walked slowly down the road, huffing and puffing. The youngest danced in front of them, singing happily.

Gradually the road grew more and

more winding, and they found themselves in a strange land where the trees were bent and twisted and the grass was dry and dusty. The sun was going down, and the sisters began to yawn.

"Time to stop," said the eldest. She pushed the youngest. "Hurry up and find some sticks. We need a fire to keep us warm. I'm going to rest." She was about to sit down when the second sister screamed.

"Eek! Don't sit there! Look at all those HORRID little ants!"

"YUCK!" The eldest jumped up. "Let's squish them and squash them!"

"NO!" The youngest came running up.

"Poor little ants!"
The eldest sister stared for a moment. Then she grinned. "All right. But only if you make us an ENORMOUS fire. AND find us something to eat! AND make us great big comfy beds!"

"That's right," said the second. "Because if you don't, we'll squash and squish EVERY SINGLE ant!"

The youngest princess scurried

around. She built a fire, and she found sweet berries and nuts and piled soft bracken and thistledown into beds for her two sisters. When the two princesses were fast asleep and snoring loudly, she sat down with a sigh.

"Thank you, princess," said a teeny-weeny voice.

The youngest princess looked all around. There was a tickle on her arm, and she saw an ant standing there, bowing.

"Thank you for your kindness. If ever you have need of help, call for the king of the ants, and I will help you!"

The two elder sisters were late getting up the next day. They said that it was the youngest's fault for making their beds too soft, and they began arguing about where they should begin to look for fortunes and spells and princes.

"There certainly won't be anything around here," said the eldest. "There's nothing but boring old bushes and trees."

"No," agreed the second. "And boring old rushes and reeds."

"Rushes?" said the youngest. "Then there must be a stream!" And she ran to look.

"QUACK! QUACK!" A duck flew up into the air from underneath her feet. A flurry of ducklings scattered and hopped into the stream that was hidden under the bushes.

"QUICK!" shouted the eldest sister. "Catch them! We can have delicious duck for breakfast!"

"And duckling pie for supper!" said the second.

"NO! NO!" said the youngest princess. "Dear little ducklings!"

Her two sisters stopped and looked at each other.

"Hmm," said the eldest. "What will you do for us if we leave the ducks alone?"

"I'll make you breakfast! And supper! And soft, comfy beds!"

"Well . . ." said the second.

"I PROMISE!" said the youngest.

When the two eldest sisters had eaten their breakfast, they lay down again. The youngest princess sat beside the stream, watching the fluffy yellow ducklings bobbing on the ripples.

"QUACK!" said a duck, stepping out of the reeds. "Thank you, princess. If ever you need my help, just call for the king of the ducks!"

By the end of the day, all three princesses were tired and hungry.

They walked away from the stream and up and over a hill, and their feet were sore, and their clothes were dusty.

"I can't walk a step farther," said the eldest princess.

"Nor me," said the second, and they flumped down on the ground under a tall tree. The youngest sat down too, but her sisters pulled her hair.

"We want our supper!" they demanded. "And we want it NOW!"

The youngest got slowly to her feet. There was a faint buzzing, and they all looked up.

Hanging from a branch of the tree right above them was a bees' nest.

"HONEY!" The eldest princess began shaking the branch. The bees buzzed angrily.

"HONEY!" said the second, and she shook the youngest princess. "Quick! Climb up and get us some honey! Beat down the nest! Do it NOW!"

"NO! NO! NO!" said the youngest. "Leave the bees! Please leave the bees!"

But her sisters would not listen to her. They hurried to find long sticks and came crashing back through the woods waving them.

"NO!" said the youngest. "NO!" And she climbed up the tree and held the bees' nest in her arms. Bees flew all around her, but not one stung her.

The two eldest sisters looked at each other and threw down their sticks.

"You'd better promise us something VERY special," said the second.

"VERY special indeed!" said the eldest.

"I'll find the fortunes!" promised the youngest princess. "I'll break the spells! I'll find the princes!"

"Very well," said the eldest sister.
"But you'd better be quick about it!"

"That's right," said the second.
"We're TIRED of questing!"

That night, the youngest sister could
not sleep. She climbed right up to the
top of the tree and looked out over
the starlit land. The bees hummed
around her, and a small voice buzzed
in her ear.

"Thank you, princess! Thank you!

If ever you have need of us, call for the queen of the bees!"

The youngest sister smiled. "I'll remember." She climbed a little higher and stopped. What was that she could see outlined against the night sky? She rubbed her eyes. It looked like a castle. . . .

The two eldest sisters were not pleased at being woken up.

"Quick!" called the youngest sister. "I can see a castle! It must be the end of our quest!"

The three princesses reached the castle as the sun began to rise. The eldest knocked loudly on the door,

and a little old woman opened it.
"We've come to find our fortunes
and break the spells and rescue
the princes, old hag!" said
the eldest princess rudely.
"So let us in!"
said the second.
The old woman
nodded. She led them
inside and showed them
a courtyard full of tall grass
and weeds. All around were
stone statues . . . statues of
princesses. They looked
surprised and angry—and

very, very still.

"Excuse me," said the youngest princess, "but what are these?"

The old woman cackled. "Princesses, my dear," she said. "Come questing, they did, but they couldn't break the spell. The spell caught them instead!"

The two eldest princesses took a step back and pushed the youngest forward. "SHE'S going to do the spell-breaking," they said. "SHE'S the one who'll get turned to stone if she fails!"

The little old woman cackled again. "Too late, my dears! If she fails, you ALL get turned to stone!"

The two eldest turned around to run, but the door was firmly shut. They glared at the youngest. "You'd better get it right!"

The youngest sighed. "Where do I begin?"

The little old woman pointed to the grassy courtyard.

"Hidden in here are a thousand pearls," she said. "Find them all, and that's your fortune. Fail, and you'll be turned to stone!"

"And then?" asked the youngest.

The little old woman took her arm. "Look here," she said.

The youngest daughter looked down and saw a deep, dark well, full of gleaming water.

"At the bottom is a golden key," said the old woman. "Find it, or you'll all be turned to stone."

"And then?" asked the youngest.

The old woman rubbed her hands together. "Then we'll see what we'll see! But you'll never find the key!" And she shuffled away.

The two eldest
princesses sat down
and burst into tears.

"We don't want to be turned to
stone!" they wailed. "We want to go
HOME!"

The youngest took no notice. She
sat down among the poppies
and daisies and called,
"King of the ants! King of
the ants! I need you!"

Almost at once there was a faint
rustling among the long grasses as
ants came hurrying and
scurrying out from all around.
They came in twos

and threes and fours and carried with them the shimmering pearls.

The youngest daughter sat and counted, and in only an hour all of the pearls were piled at her feet.

"Thank you, thank you!" she called as the ants scurried away.

The old woman was not pleased at the youngest princess's success. She grunted as she took her to the well, but the princess smiled as she knelt down beside the water.

"King of the ducks! King of the ducks! I need you!"

QUAAAAAAAAAAACK!

There was a flurry and flapping of

wings, and the king of the ducks
landed with a loud splash. He
winked at the youngest princess and
dived deep, deep down into the well.
In no time, she had the dripping
golden key on her lap.

"Thank you, thank you, king of
the ducks!" she called as the duck
beat his wings and flew away.

The old woman took the key.

"You must come this way," she said and unlocked a huge golden door. The youngest princess followed her, and the two eldest princesses came behind, sniffling.

Behind the golden door was a huge golden hall, and in the hall was a huge stone bed. Lying in the bed were three princes, as like each other as three peas.

The two eldest princesses clapped their hands as they stared.

"So HANDSOME!" whispered the eldest.

The second sister pinched the youngest. "Wake them up!"

The old woman cackled again. "Not

so fast! Stone they are, and stone you'll
be if you choose wrong!" She turned
to the youngest princess. "One ate
sugar, one ate syrup, and the youngest
ate honey before they were enchanted!
Now, choose the youngest!"

The youngest princess walked slowly
over to the bed.

"Queen of the bees!" she
whispered. "Queen of the bees!"

There was a gentle humming, and in

through the open window zigzagged the queen of the bees. She flew over the three princes and settled on the closest. The youngest princess sat down on the bed and put out her hand.

"This is the youngest prince!" she said.

At once there was a rush of wind and the sound of hurrying feet and chattering voices as the stone princesses leaped back to life. They burst into the golden hall, but as they did so, the bed gave a hop and a skip and a jump and soared up and out a window. The two eldest princesses were only just in time to snatch at

the covers and hang on tightly.

The king and the queen and the prime minister were walking in the royal garden when the bed landed with a THUMP! beside them. The two eldest princesses picked themselves up and dusted themselves down. The youngest was still sitting on the bed, holding the hand of the youngest prince. They were smiling happily at each other.

"Well, well!" said the prime minister. "Welcome back!"

"We've found our fortunes!" said the eldest princess, and she tipped the thousand pearls out of her pockets.

"AND our princes!" said the second, pointing to the bed.

The two eldest princes sat up and bowed.

"So glad to meet you," they said and then lay down again.

"Aren't they HANDSOME?" said the eldest princess proudly.

"Indeed we are," said the eldest prince. "We are as handsome as the moon and the sun together!"

"Exactly so," said the second prince. "And now—bring us our breakfasts!"

The King of the Blue Lagoon

Ann Turnbull

When Sally was
at the seaside,
she found a
stone on the
beach. It was
gray and oval and
smoothed by the waves,
and it just filled the palm of
her hand. Sally knew at once that it

was a magic stone. She kept it in her pocket.

One day when Sally was jumping rope in the school playground, the stone bounced out of her pocket and fell—*plop!*—into a puddle.

The puddle changed. It changed from a gray rainy-day puddle to a pool of deep, deep blue, with pink rocks in it and glinting fish that flicked between them. Sally heard the boom and hiss of the surf. She put her hand into the water. It was warm, and she felt a tickle of fish.

Her stone lay on the bottom. Sally took it out, and at once the blue sea, the surf, the pink rocks, and the glinting fish all vanished. And from Sally's hand came a voice that sighed:

"Far from the coral caves,

Far from the sea,

A witch's magic has enchanted me."

Sally put the stone back in her pocket. She looked around. No one else had noticed.

When she got home, she took the stone into the garden. In the garden was a pond, with rocks around the edge and a plastic gnome fishing on the side.

Sally put the stone into the pond.

The water turned deep, deep blue, the rocks became a coral reef, and the gnome turned into a mermaid who

combed her hair and sang wild songs.

Sally took out the stone.

The blue sea, the coral reef, and the mermaid all vanished, and Sally heard a voice that sighed:

"Far from the coral caves,
   Far from the sea,
   A witch's magic has enchanted me."
That night, Sally put the stone
into her bath.

The bath water turned
deep, deep blue. The
bath foam turned to
sea foam. The soap
became an angelfish.
The washcloth became
a manta ray. An island with
palm trees grew out of the
soap dish. On Sally's plastic
boat a pirate crew hoisted the Jolly
Roger. Sally launched a Spanish

galleon, laden with gold. There was a battle, and a cannon boomed across the water.

And all the time the stone lay on the bottom of the bathtub, and Sally's mother hadn't noticed anything.

Sally took out the stone. At once the blue sea, the angelfish, the Spaniards, and the pirates all vanished, and she heard a voice that sighed:

"Far from the coral caves,
Far from the sea,
A witch's magic has enchanted me."

After that, Sally always put the stone into her bath. But although the water changed and the boats changed and

the soap and the soap dish changed, the stone never changed. It lay on the bottom, cold and sad, and when Sally took it out, it always sighed:
 "Far from the coral caves,
    Far from the sea,
    A witch's magic has enchanted me."
One day Sally went to the seaside again. She took the stone with her.

Sally waded into the sea, holding the stone in her cupped hands. She squatted, and the sea washed over the stone and rocked it against her fingers.

The sea was a gray, cold sea. Sally thought it would change, but it didn't. Nothing changed. The sea

was gray; the
rocks were gray;
the sky was gray.

But suddenly,
in Sally's hands, the stone came alive.
It twitched. It wiggled. It slithered
and slipped. Sally looked down and
saw that the stone had changed into a
fish: a bright, bright fish with a rose-
red body and turquoise stripes, golden
eyes with black rims, fins that flicked
silver, and a rose-red, shimmering tail.
On its head was a crown.

"Oh!" said Sally. She was so
surprised that she opened her
fingers, and the fish slipped through.

Before she could catch it, it flicked
its tail and wiggled its body and swam
away, as bright as a jewel in the gray
sea. Sally watched it grow smaller and
smaller until at last it was no bigger
than a sequin. Then it disappeared.

Sally felt something scraping and
bumping against her foot. She bent
down and picked up a shell. It was a
big shell, pale pink and spiraled, that
looked as if it had
come from a blue
sea far away.

Sally waded
back to the
shore, holding

her shell. She knew at once that it was a magic shell. She showed it to her mother.

"You can hear the sea in a shell," said Sally's mother.

Sally held the shell to her ear. She heard the sea. She heard the boom and hiss of far-off surf. And above the sound of the surf she heard a glad voice, singing:

"Deep in the coral caves,
Under the sea,
King of the blue lagoon,
now I am free."

Tom Thumb

Joyce Dunbar

A woodcutter was chopping logs in his yard while his wife threw corn to the chickens. "If only we had a child to play around us," he said, "then we would be really happy."

"I couldn't agree more," said his wife. "Why, if I could have one small son, even no bigger than my thumb, I would be the happiest woman alive."

Now, it so happened that the fairies heard them and decided to grant their wish. Not long after, the woodcutter's wife had a tiny child, not much bigger than her thumb. He could walk and talk in no time, and the fairies made him a suit of clothes. His hat was made of an oak leaf, his shirt spun out of spiders' webs, his jacket woven from thistledown, and his pants from feathers.

His mother and father were overjoyed. "We have what we wished for," they said, "and we will always love him dearly." They named him Tom Thumb.

Even though Tom was so little, he was as merry and mischievous as any child could be. "Can I help you plow the fields, Father?" he asked one day.

"Why, no, you are much too small to ride a horse, Tom," said his father.

"Oh, no, I'm not," said Tom. "Just set me in the horse's ear." His father did so. "Whoa, steady," said Tom, straight into the horse's ear. All went well until Tom decided to go for a gallop. "Giddyap!" he suddenly yelled, so that the horse ran through the town, upturning all of the market stands on the main street.

"You are a bad boy, Tom Thumb," said his father when he caught up with him. "You will never make your way in the world if you play tricks like that."

Even so, he let Tom ride home in his favorite place, on the rim of his hat, for his son was the apple of his eye.

"Can I help you mix the batter for the pudding?" Tom asked his mother on another day.

"But, Tom, you are too small," she replied.

"Oh, no, I'm not," said Tom. "Just set me on the table."

But no sooner was her back turned than Tom decided to go boating on the bowl of batter in half an eggshell.

The eggshell upturned, tipping Tom Thumb into the mixture. He kicked and thrashed around and might have drowned if his mother hadn't fished him out in time.

"What am I going to do with you?" she said. "I don't see how you will ever make your way in the world."

Even so, she kissed him and washed him in a teacup, for her son was her pride and joy.

Soon after, Tom's mother took him out milking in the meadow. He sneaked out of her apron pocket and ran down a snail shell. "Here I am!" he called. Then he hid down a

mouse hole.
"Here I am!" he
called. Then
he crept under a
stone, still calling,
"Here I am!"

This time his
mother caught him
and tied him to a thistle
with a fine thread so that she
might continue with her
milking. But the cow thought
that she saw a tasty morsel and
took Tom and the thistle up in
one mouthful. Around and
around he was tumbled, with the

cow's huge teeth chewing and grinding. "Here I am, Mother!" he cried out in terror.

"You're a wicked little boy, Tom Thumb," she replied. "I cannot play hide-and-seek all morning." And she went on with her milking.

"Mother, please come and get me!" yelled Tom, so loudly that his voice tickled the cow's tonsils, and he was coughed up into the long grass. He began waving his arms so wildly that a raven swept him up and dropped him into the sea, where he was swallowed by an enormous fish.

Luckily, the fish was caught soon after and presented to a king for his supper. What a shock everyone got when out popped Tom Thumb!

The king was delighted with him. He gave him a mouse with a saddle to ride on and a sewing needle for a sword. Tom charged around scaring spiders away from the three princesses, so they made him their champion knight.

But Tom was missing his father and mother. "You will go home to see them," said the king, "and you will take

all the treasures that you can carry."

They made him a golden coach from a walnut shell, with four silver buttons for wheels and six mice to pull it.

Tom set off home with all of his treasures, which was a single gold coin. But it took him all day just to reach the edge of the palace grounds. "Not to worry," said the princesses. "We have some presents from the fairies that will help you to find your way home."

The first princess gave him an enchanted hat, which shrank to fit the wearer's head and showed him whatever was going on in all parts of the world. The second gave him a pair of boots, which shrank to fit the wearer's feet and could in a moment carry him to all corners of the earth. The third gave him a precious ring, which he wore around his waist like a girdle, giving him the strength of a giant.

Tom Thumb put on the hat and saw his mother and father weeping for the loss of him. So he put on the boots and wished that he was home.

"Here I am, Mother!" he cried. "See, Father! I have made my way in the world!"

And to show that he had the strength of a giant, he lifted them up in his arms before giving them such a big hug!

The Enchanted Princess

Judy Hindley

A beautiful princess named Gloriana was riding in the mountains with her younger sisters. Suddenly, she saw a wonderful deer with eyes like stars. . . .

"Catch me if you can!" called the deer.

The princess and her sisters followed the deer. They galloped and galloped as fast as they could go. But however fast they went, the deer was always just ahead.

At last, the poor horses could go no farther.

"Let's turn back!" cried Gloriana's sisters. But Gloriana wouldn't stop.

Finally, the little sisters could go no farther.

"Please turn back!" they called to Gloriana. But even then, she wouldn't stop.

On and on she went, until at last she couldn't even hear their cries.

At that moment, the deer stood still

and waited. She ran toward it.

"I am a magician," said the deer. "Do you have any wishes?"

"Oh, yes!" cried Gloriana. "I want to be rich and live in a splendid castle with fine new clothes and jewels."

"What about your sisters?" asked the deer. "I heard them calling you."

"Never mind my sisters," said Gloriana. "They're always calling and running after me. This time, let them find their own way home."

"Very well, then," said the deer. "You have your wish. But someday, you will call, and they won't hear. Oh, my dear, you will cry and cry, until you are as kind as you are beautiful."

Suddenly, the deer was gone, and Gloriana stood on the steps of a shining castle.

That night, Gloriana ate from a golden plate and drank from a golden cup. She went to sleep in a golden bed as big as a boat.

When she woke up, she found rooms full of jewels and fine new clothes. Now she had everything she wanted—but there was no one to see it and no one to share it with.

Time went by. Soon the splendid castle seemed very lonely.

One day, Gloriana said, "I'll ask my

sisters to come and stay with me. They always do what I want."

Away she went along the mountain road.

At last, she saw her sisters in a meadow.

"Sisters, sisters, come with me!" she cried. She jumped off her horse to run to them.

But as soon as her feet touched the ground, she turned into a small gray rabbit.

"Look! What a dear little

rabbit!" cried her sisters. As they played with her, she tried to talk to them, but they couldn't hear a single word. .

Just before sunset, they waved goodbye and went away.

As soon as they had left, Gloriana became a princess once again. But it was too late—she had to go back alone to her grand castle.

"That mountain must be bewitched!" said Gloriana. The next day, away she went, by the river road.

This time, she saw her sisters by the riverbank.

"Sisters, sisters, come with me!" she cried.

Again, she jumped off her horse to run to them. But as soon as her feet touched the riverbank, she turned into a little golden fish.

"Look! What a pretty fish!" cried her sisters.

They leaned out over the river to try to see her. She leaped up high to try to speak to them. But of course, they couldn't hear a single word.

This time, Gloriana cried and cried, but her tears ran into the river, and no one saw them.

At sunset, her sisters went away. Once again, Gloriana went back alone to her grand castle.

"Perhaps the river is bewitched," said Gloriana. So the next day she rode into the forest.

The forest was dark and gloomy. Gloriana was frightened. But she went on.

Suddenly, the wonderful deer ran across her path. Her sisters came chasing after it with a hunter. They were galloping, galloping, straight toward a cliff.

"Stop, stop!" called Gloriana. She

jumped from her horse
to stand in front of
them. But this time
she turned into a big
white bear. And when
she called, her voice
was a great roar.

They stopped—and
the hunter raised his
bow and shot her.

Down fell the bear, still roaring. As
it fell, its roar became the sweet voice
of the princess.

The hunter raised his bow to shoot
again. But the little princesses heard
their sister's voice.

"No!" they cried. "Don't shoot! It's Gloriana!"

They ran to hug the wounded bear, and its eyes filled with tears.

Then a voice said, "Don't cry, Gloriana." There stood the wonderful deer with eyes like stars. It said, "You risked your life to save your sisters— you have become as kind as you are beautiful."

And as the deer spoke, Gloriana again became a princess.

Then, suddenly, the deer was gone, and the sisters stood on the steps of the shining castle, where they stayed together all of their long and happy lives.

Acknowledgments

"The Three Wishes," "Tom Thumb," and "The Wonder Broom" reproduced by permission of The Agency (London) Ltd. copyright © **Joyce Dunbar** 1993. First published by Kingfisher in *The Kingfisher Read-Aloud Storybook*; "Chantelle, the Princess Who Couldn't Sing" reproduced by permission of The Agency (London) Ltd. copyright © **Joyce Dunbar** 1997. First published by Kingfisher in *Breaking the Spell: Tales of Enchantment*; "The Queen of the Bees" taken from *Breaking the Spell: Tales of Enchantment* (Kingfisher) by **Vivian French** copyright © Vivian French 1997; "The Enchanted Princess" and "The Magical Apple Tree" taken from *My Own Fairy Story Book* (Kingfisher) by **Judy Hindley** copyright © Judy Hindley 1991; "The Cletterkin" taken from *Stories for the Very Young* (Kingfisher) by **Jenny Koralek** copyright © Jenny Koralek 1989; "The Hedley Kow" taken from *Time for Telling* (Kingfisher) by **Maggie Pearson** copyright © Maggie Pearson 1991; "Baby Wizard" taken from *Bedtime Stories for the Very Young* (Kingfisher) by **Chris Powling** copyright © Chris Powling 1991; "The King of the Blue Lagoon" taken from *Bedtime Stories for the Very Young* (Kingfisher) by **Ann Turnbull** copyright © Ann Turnbull 1991.